Paddington

the Artist

MICHAEL BOND

Paddington

the Artist

illustrated by R.W. ALLEY

HarperCollins *Children's Books*

One Sunday Paddington was out for a walk
with his friend Mr Gruber, when they came
across some paintings tied to the railings
outside the park.

"It's what is known as an Outdoor
Exhibition," said Mr Gruber. "They have
one here every week when the weather
is nice."

"All the paintings are for sale," Mr Gruber
explained. "This one is called 'Sunset in
Bombay'."

"I'm glad I don't live in Bombay," said
Paddington. "It might keep me awake
all night."

"How about this one then?" said Mr Gruber.
"It's called 'Storm at Sea'."

Paddington suddenly wished he hadn't
eaten such a big breakfast.

"I feel sick," he said, and he hurried on to
the next picture.

"This is a picture the artist painted of himself," said Mr Gruber. "It's called a self-portrait. I think it looks very like him."

Paddington gave the picture a hard stare.

"I don't think I'll buy any paintings today, Mr Gruber," he said.

Paddington looked very thoughtful as he made his way back home to number thirty-two Windsor Gardens.

When he got there, Paddington collected all
his paints and brushes from his room and
went out into the garden.

The next Sunday, when he and Mr Gruber had finished their walk, Paddington led the way back towards Windsor Gardens.

"I'm having an Outdoor Exhibition of my own this week, Mr Gruber," he said.

"This is meant to be a sunset in Windsor Gardens. Only it took me quite a long time and it got dark before I could finish it.

"And this is a picture of a rainstorm, only it got very wet and all the paint ran."

"This is my best one," said Paddington. "It's a picture of me. I've put my special paw mark on to show I painted it myself."

Mr Gruber gazed at Paddington's portrait for a long time.

"It is very good, Mr Brown," he said at last, not wishing to upset his friend, "but I think you look even better in real life."

"I kept going upstairs to look at myself in the mirror," said Paddington, "but by the time I got downstairs again I'd forgotten what I looked like."

"Painting isn't as easy as it looks,"
Paddington added sadly, "especially with
paws. I think I might give up."

"I hope you don't do that, Mr Brown,"
Mr Gruber said thoughtfully.

After Mr Gruber had said goodbye,
Paddington sat down beside his paintings
hoping that someone would stop and
buy one.

But it was a warm day and no one came
past. In the end Paddington fell asleep.

When he woke up, Paddington found to his surprise that all his pictures had gone.

But tucked inside his duffle coat he found an envelope with his name on: Mr Paddington Brown, 32 Windsor Gardens. And inside the envelope there was some money and a note saying 'Thank you'.

If Mr and Mrs Brown recognised Mr
Gruber's writing they didn't say anything.
They hadn't had such a peaceful time
for ages.

And best of all, Paddington carried on
painting. So everyone was happy.

"I think I may paint a family portrait now,"
said Paddington. "That is, if I have enough
paint left for all the smiles."

First published in hardback in Great Britain by HarperCollins*Publishers* in 1985
First published in paperback by Collins Picture Books in 2000
Published as part of a gift set by HarperCollins Children's Books in 2007

1 3 5 7 9 10 8 6 4 2

Collins Picture Books is an imprint of the Children's Division, part of HarperCollins Publishers Ltd.
HarperCollins Children's Books is a division of HarperCollins Publishers Ltd.

Visit our website at: www.harpercollinschildrensbooks.co.uk

Printed and bound in China